Growing up in Kakadu
AUSTRALIA

Story by Stan Breeden
Pictures by Belinda Wright

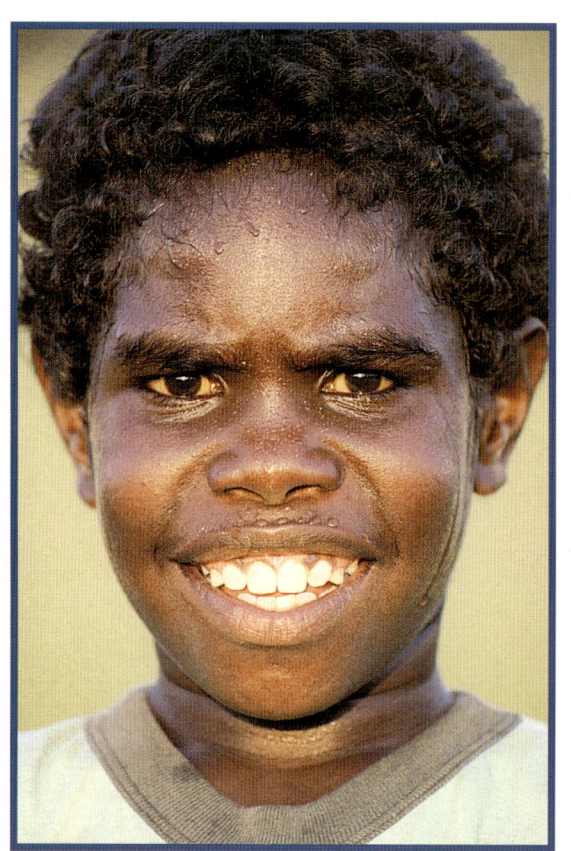 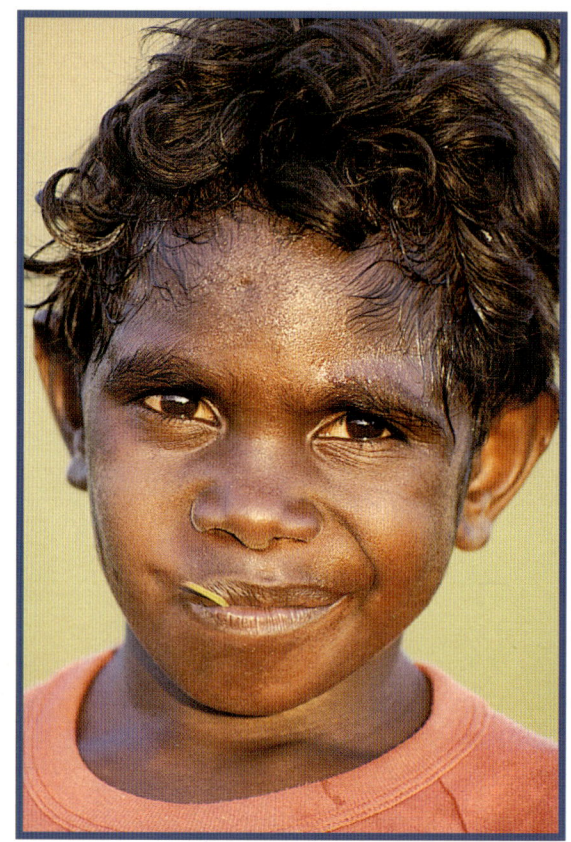

James and Simon live with their families and friends in Kakadu. They call themselves Gagudju people. The children learn about plants and animals from their elders.

They also learn about the sacred places. They are told that some of the sacred places are secret. They must not go into them until they are grown up. Dangerous spirits live there that will carry children away.

Kakadu is a far-away and wild place.
The Gagudju people have lived there
for thousands and thousands of years.

Deep inside Kakadu are rocky cliffs, deep gorges, caves and clear pools full of fish and crocodiles.

Nipper Kapirigi is a wise old Gagudju man. He must look after a place called Djuwarr, in the stone country. He carries a spear. When he was a young man he used his spears to hunt goannas, wallabies and even fish.

Kapirigi camps at Djuwarr with his friend Minnie Gapindi. Gapindi uses the wing of a magpie goose to fan herself.

apirigi catches some fish in the waterhole. Then he walks far into the gorge. He sees many stone country animals.

A rock wallaby jumps out of his way.

Rock pigeons drink at a spring in a cave.

A rock possum peers at him from behind a boulder.

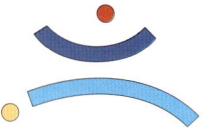

Bright flowers grow among the rocks.

Kapirigi finds the bower of a very special bird. It dances around sticks it has placed in the ground and piles of shells and bones it has gathered in the bush.

Kapirigi calls this great bowerbird Djuwe. He warns the children that the bird is dangerous. He tells them that Djuwe would like to steal their bones to put in his bower.

Kapirigi walks further and further. He comes to a wall of smooth rock covered with paintings of animals and people. Some of the paintings were made by Kapirigi's father and uncles.

The Gagudju say that if they paint the animals these will be in Kakadu for ever and ever.

There are paintings of a huge python, which is a kind of snake, black wallaroos and many others. Most of these animals live among the rocks.

Harmless freshwater crocodiles also live at Djuwarr. Kapirigi finds a nest of their eggs buried in the sand. He loves to eat them so he digs them up and takes them to his camp to share with Gapindi.

Waterfalls crash down the rocks after storms in November and December. Kapirigi tells the children that the lightning is brought by Namarrkun, the lightning man.

Namarrkun is a spirit who lives above the clouds. He carries the lightning across his shoulders. He has axes made of stone tied to his elbows and knees. With these he makes the thunder.

With the first storms, large blue and orange grasshoppers appear in hidden corners of the stone country. Kapirigi says these are Namarrkun's children.

Kapirigi and his friend Bluey Ilkirr still know how to make stone axes. By hitting a big boulder with a small one, they break off pieces of rock which are as sharp as knives.

Nowadays they do not use stone axes. They use axes and knives made of steel.

Bluey Ilkirr does not live in the stone country. His camp is among the gum trees in the forest.

In the wet season the rains keep the grass fresh and green. When the rain stops, the children run about and play with their dog.

In camp, Susan Aladjingu, Ilkirr's wife, plays cat's cradle with her friends. She makes shapes of turtles, kangaroos and even rainstorms.

Ilkirr shows the children the forest animals and tells them how they live. Goannas are very tasty. They are good bush tucker but you must run very fast to catch them.

At the end of the rainy season, the masked finch builds its nest among the grasses. The grass seeds are ripe then and are excellent food for the growing young birds.

An azure kingfisher brings a fish for its young.

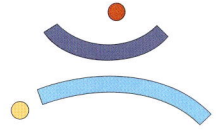

If you look carefully into a hollow tree, Ilkirr tells the children, you may surprise Lambalk, the sugar glider, asleep in its nest. It comes out in the evening to run about the treetops all night.

Ilkirr tells the children that in the Dreamtime, long, long ago, before the Gagudju lived here, animals made parts of the land. In those days, animals could become people and had many adventures.

It was then that Gurri, the blue-tongued lizard, fell on his face and bruised his tongue. It turned blue. Gurri's tongue is still blue.

Gundamen, the frilled lizard, was once a man. He was smooth and sleek. But he did the wrong thing in a ceremony. He got it all wrong because he did not listen to the elders. The elders punished Gundamen by making him rough and scaly with loose skin around his neck.

Garndagitj, the antelope kangaroo, lives in small mobs. The young males play and wrestle. In the Dreamtime, Garndagitj made rock outcrops as he moved about the land. Nearly every animal and place in Gagudju country has a story.

Bluey Ilkirr is an artist. To make one of his masterpieces, he cuts a big piece of bark from a stringybark tree. When it is dry, he cuts it into pieces to paint on. He colours the bark with paint made from a red stone called ochre. Then he paints the shapes of animals with white clay. For the fine details he uses a brush made from a grass stem.

While he paints, his wife Aladjingu looks after an orphan wallaby.

Beyond Kakadu's forests are the billabongs and swamps. The children's uncle, Jonathan Nadji, goes fishing there. He catches barramundi with his spear.

Jonathan must be careful because Ginga, the dangerous saltwater crocodile, also lives in the billabong. Ginga sometimes catches people as well as fish.

Jonathan sees a big crocodile catch a barramundi. Other crocodiles lie on the bank warming themselves in the sun.

Crocodiles are not always easy to see. They like to hide under plants that grow in the water.

The children go swimming in a safe billabong. They hide under the green plants and try to frighten their friends by pretending to be crocodiles.

Out on the plain near another billabong stands a very special rock. It is called Indjuwanydjuwa. The Gagudju people say it is one of the beings that created the Dreamtime.

Indjuwanydjuwa is a long word, difficult to say. When you say it right, In-djoo-wund-joo-wah, it sounds like a song.

The children's grandfather and Jonathan's father is Big Bill Neidjie. He is a tall man with white hair. His voice is so deep that when he says "Indjuwanydjuwa" the air vibrates.

He and his old friend Felix Iyanuk are Gagudju elders. Together they must look after Indjuwanydjuwa.

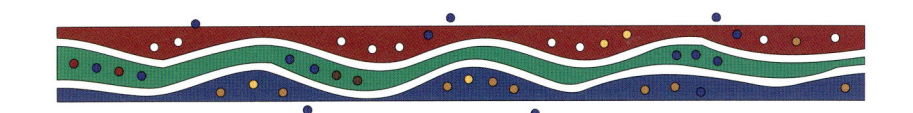

Iyanuk sings to the rock from a cave not far away. There is a painting of Indjuwanydjuwa behind him.

By singing special songs, painting on rocks and performing ceremonies, the Gagudju people make sure that Kakadu never changes. This way the birds, waterlilies, kangaroos, crocodiles, fish, lizards and all the other plants and animals will always be there. And the people will always be there too.

Neidjie tells the children that the white-breasted sea-eagle is the boss of the billabongs and swamps. He calls it Marrawuti. You must never harm this great bird, he warns them.

Marrawuti and his mate have built a huge nest in a paperbark tree.

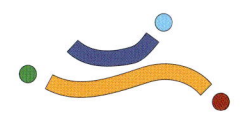

They have two dark-brown young in the nest.

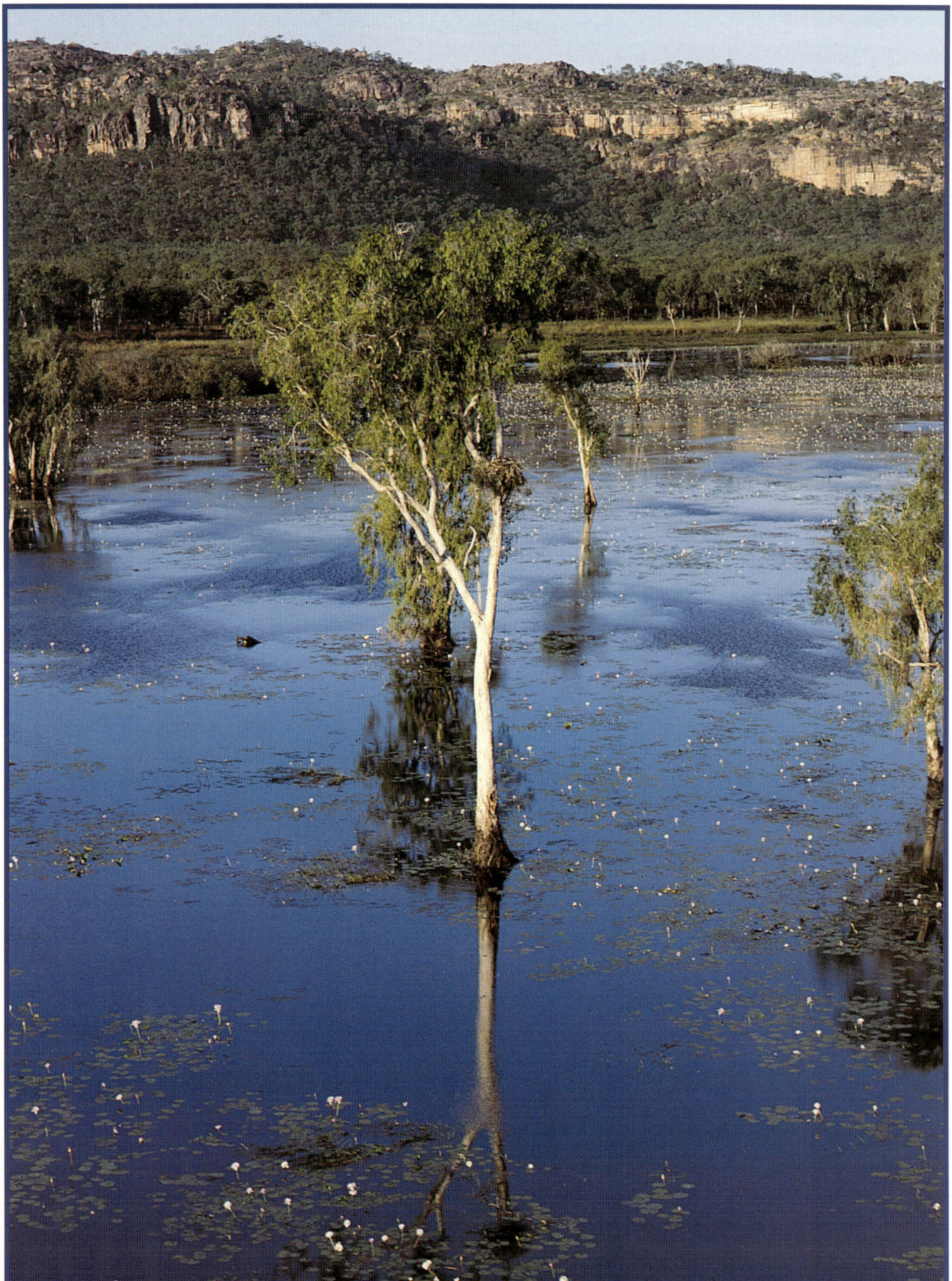

Below Marrawuti's nest live other waterbirds. Pelicans rest and a masked plover walks along the muddy edge of the swamp.

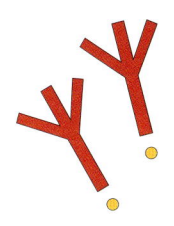

A lotusbird looks after its eggs.
A black-necked stork catches a water snake.
A whistle-duck lands.
A magpie goose scratches its chin.

Everywhere there are birds, birds, birds.

To learn more about his country, Jonathan talks with Neidjie, his father. The two visit special places.

To show he belongs to the country, Jonathan puts a picture of his hand on the rocks. First he puts his hand on the stone. Then he blows a mixture of white clay and water from his mouth all over his hand. When he takes his hand away, the picture is left behind.

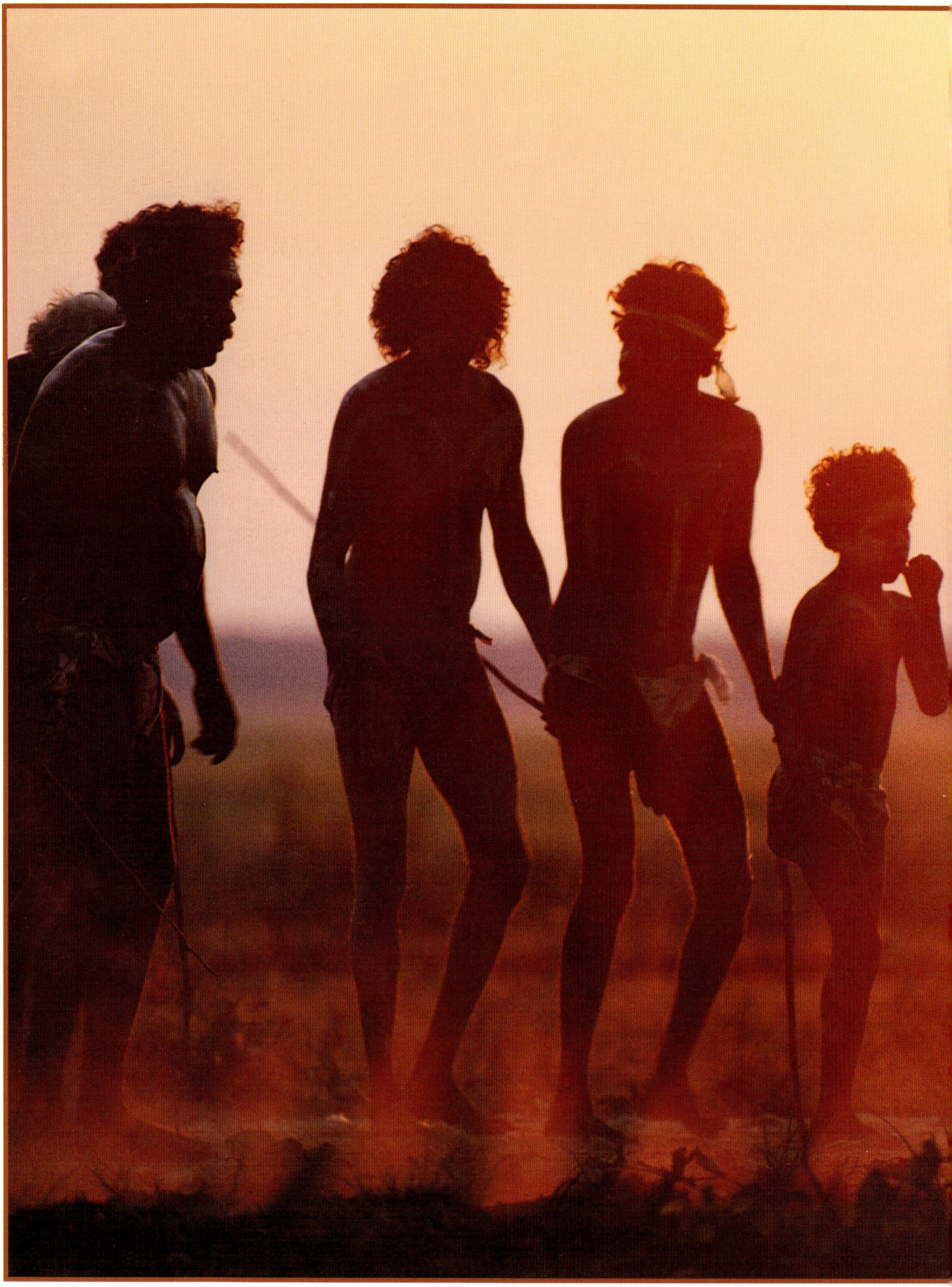

One day, men come from another place for a special ceremony. They paint themselves and they paint James too. They all sing and dance. James dances with them and so he learns the songs and special moves.

Playing, listening to the older people, doing what his older brothers and uncles do, he and the other boys slowly learn the ways of the Gagudju.

The girls learn many of the same things but they also have their own special Dreamtime stories and their own ceremonies.

By listening to the stories and joining in the ceremonies, the boys and girls learn how to become proper Gagudju men and women.